Doctor Dolittle

and the Lighthouse

RED FOX READ ALONE

Red Fox Read Alones are fab first readers! With funny stories and cool illustrations, reading's never been so much fun!

Based on the stories by
HUGH LOFTING
Retold by Alison Sage

Doctor Dolittle
and the Lighthouse

Illustrated by Sarah Wimperis

RED FOX

A Red Fox Book

Published by Random House Children's Books
20 Vauxhall Bridge Road, London SW1V 2SA

A division of The Random House Group Ltd
London Melbourne Sydney Auckland
Johannesburg and agencies throughout the world

Text based on *Doctor Dolittle's Post Office*
Copyright, 1923, by Hugh Lofting
Copyright, 1950, by Josephine Lofting
Copyright, 1988, by Christopher Lofting

1 3 5 7 9 10 8 6 4 2

This Read Alone Novel first published in Great Britain
by Red Fox 2000

The Random House Group Limited supports The Forest Stewardship
Council (FSC®), the leading international forest certification organisation.
Our books carrying the FSC label are printed on FSC® certified paper.
FSC is the only forest certification scheme endorsed by the leading
environmental organisations, including Greenpeace. Our
paper procurement policy can be found at
www.randomhouse.co.uk/environment

Printed and bound in Great Britain by Clays Ltd, St Ives PLC

The Random House Group Limited Reg. No. 954009

www.randomhouse.co.uk

ISBN 0 09 940432 X

MIX
Paper from
responsible sources
FSC® C018072

Contents

Doctor Dolittle at Home

Once, many years ago, there lived a man called Doctor Dolittle.

He wasn't rich and he wasn't famous – at least, he wasn't famous amongst people. But he was known everywhere by animals. The animals loved and respected him because he was the best doctor they had ever known. He had even learned animal languages. This meant he could talk to sick creatures and find out just what was the matter with them.

Doctor Dolittle lived in a little white house in Puddleby-on-the-Marsh, together with his animal friends.

There was Dab-Dab
the duck,

Jip the dog,

Gub-Gub the baby pig,

Too-Too the owl

and a little white
mouse called Whitey.

He also had a very rare creature –
a two-headed pushmi-pullyu – who

had come to live with Doctor Dolittle years before, after the Doctor went to Africa to help some very sick monkeys.

You might wonder how Doctor Dolittle found the time to care for sick creatures, if he was looking after so many animals at home. But all his little animal family helped in the house, and they were each very clever at doing their own jobs.

Jip was in charge of cleaning, and every day he would sweep his tail over the floors with a rag tied on it for a broom.

Dab-Dab looked after the house-keeping and saw that there was enough food in the cupboards and that they weren't running out of the Doctor's favourite ginger biscuits.

She was clever at remembering things and she would always have the Doctor's umbrella ready if it looked like rain.

Too-Too was good at adding up and he did all of the sums, so the Doctor always knew if he was running out of money. Which he often was.

Gub-Gub was too little to do very much, but he did try hard to look after the garden. The only problem was, he sometimes ate the vegetables when nobody was looking.

Whitey, the white mouse, was useful at finding things. The animals had only to say, 'I wonder where I put my book,' or 'I've lost my packet of mints,' for him to start scurrying hither and thither until he found them.

The pushmi-pullyu liked to do the shopping. At first he hated going out because everyone stared at his two heads. Sometimes farmers in carts would shout at him when he tried to cross the road because they weren't sure if he was coming or going. That made him blush bright pink and want to hide one of his heads in the shopping basket. But after a while, all the shops in Puddleby got to know him and the greengrocer often put aside a few bananas. Bananas were his favourite food.

'I don't know how I managed without you all,' the Doctor would say. 'The house is the cleanest and best run in Puddleby.'

Dab-Dab has an Idea

While the animals were looking after the house, Doctor Dolittle was busy curing sick animals, who came in a steady stream to see him. Sometimes, by the time he was ready to start work, the queue stretched all the way round the garden and back into the road.

The Doctor never complained, even though he often didn't finish until late in the evening. 'Someone has got to look after all these animals,' he would say.

But Dab-Dab couldn't help noticing how tired he looked.

Then one day the Doctor fell asleep at the breakfast table.

Dab-Dab was terribly worried. 'He works so hard, he'll make himself ill,' she said to the other animals.

'He needs a holiday,' said Too-Too.

When the Doctor came downstairs the next day, all the animals were huddled over a brightly coloured book.

'What's that?' asked the Doctor.

'Nothing,' said Dab-Dab quickly.

'Oh, but it is!' said Gub-Gub. 'It's a lovely book of places to go— erf, schlump.'

Jip had shoved a large piece of toast in the piglet's mouth.

'You see, Doctor,' said Dab-Dab firmly. 'We think it's about time we had a holiday. It's ages since we went to Africa and all of us would love a change of air.'

'But there's so much to do, here!' said the Doctor. 'I couldn't possibly go away.' Then he yawned and started to put salt on his porridge instead of sugar.

'See?' said Dab-Dab crossly. 'You must listen to us and take a break.'

'Perhaps you're right,' admitted the Doctor. 'I am a bit tired. But only for a week or so, mind.'

Later that day, there was great excitement as he and Too-Too took down the old money box and started working out how much it would cost to go away for a holiday.

Doctor Dolittle on Holiday

Once he had made up his mind to have a holiday, the Doctor could hardly wait. Where should they go? Everyone had a different idea and they all began talking at once. The Doctor put his hands over his ears.

'Shh! everyone!' he said. 'There's only enough money for a week at the seaside. What do you think of that?'

'Yes! Yes!' everyone shouted very happily.

Straightaway they all began to think about packing, because the Doctor said they should go the next Saturday.

Too-Too booked seats on the early morning stagecoach. Dab-Dab washed all their clothes and Jip ironed them. Whitey found all sorts of useful things to take, like a rubber ball and a windbreak (in case the wind blew sand in their picnic). The pushmi-pullyu made lots of shopping trips to buy everything they needed, and Gub-Gub tried to help but he ran about squealing and getting in everyone's way.

'That pig!' grumbled Jip to Dab-Dab. 'One of these days he's going to get his bottom nipped.' Jip had packed his case full of bones and Gub-Gub had tripped over it and sent everything flying.

When the Doctor saw the bones he told Jip to leave them behind. 'There'll be plenty of food where we're going,' he said

'The Doctor understands almost everything about us animals,' said Jip to Dab-Dab, 'but he doesn't realise how much I love an old bone, well buried. New bones just aren't the same.'

The Swallow Arrives

Saturday came and at last they were ready. They set off to meet the stagecoach and everyone was in a very good mood. As they sat in the sunshine, waiting for the coach, the pushmi-pullyu saw a cloud of swallows flying high overhead.

'It really is summer,' he said. 'The swallows have arrived from Africa.'

And he looked a little bit sad.

The Doctor smiled at him. 'And one day, we'll all go back there ourselves. But now we are going to have a good time at the seaside, aren't we?'

The pushmi-pullyu was just about to say something, when suddenly there was a whoosh of wings and a swallow landed on a gatepost next to them.

'Hello, Doctor!' twittered the swallow. 'Remember me? I went on your last trip to Africa. I thought it was you.'

'How nice to see you!' said the Doctor and the swallow started chatting about his family.

'But where are your friends?' said the Doctor. 'Don't get left behind!'

'What, me? Never. I know just where they're going. They're going to Little Snoring on Sea. We go there every year at this time. Lovely little place.'

'Why, that's where we're going,' said the Doctor.

Just then they heard the coach rumbling round the corner. The animals jumped up excitedly and began sorting out their luggage.

'I'll be off then, Doctor,' said the swallow, 'but I'll see you in Little Snoring. Have a safe journey.'

The Animals Set Off

When the coach arrived, Doctor Dolittle and all the animals scrambled aboard.

The coachman put his head in at the door to check the tickets, but when he saw all the animals sitting on the seats he got quite a shock.

'No livestock, no fish, no birds and definitely no wild animals,' he said crossly, looking at Too-Too and Gub-Gub in a very nasty way.

The Doctor pointed out that none of the animals were in the least bit wild, and in any case, they all had tickets. Then the pushmi-pullyu, who had been sitting quietly in the corner, leaned over to see what was the matter. He lowered his horns at the coachman. 'Shall I tip him off the coach?' he asked the Doctor.

'Goodness me, no!' cried Doctor Dolittle in alarm.

Things could have become very difficult, but a nice girl said she didn't mind if the Doctor's animals stayed on the coach. She had never travelled with an owl and a pig and a two-headed creature before, she said, but they seemed very well behaved. The coachman scowled, but in the end he let them stay and the journey began.

When he had gone, the animals opened their packed lunches. The pushmi-pullyu politely offered the nice girl one of his bananas.

'Thank you very much,' she said, smiling.

Then the Doctor asked Gub-Gub if he wanted a drink.

The girl looked at the Doctor, her

eyes as wide as saucers. 'Were you talking to that little pig?' she asked.

The Doctor laughed and explained that he could understand animal languages.

'How clever you are!' she said, and she asked the Doctor where he was travelling to.

'But that's where I'm going!' she cried when he told her. 'I'm visiting my aunt. She's got a huge house looking out over the sea. My name's Dora, by the way. I thought I was going to have a very dull week but now it won't be boring at all.'

They all talked non-stop for the rest of the journey and when they arrived at Little Snoring, they set off together towards the seafront.

'It's not far,' explained Dora. 'My aunt keeps a little rowing boat moored in front your hotel. It's called the *Lucky Lucy*. I'll take you out in it if you like.'

'We'd love that,' said the Doctor, as they said goodbye outside the hotel.

* * *

'This is so *exciting*!' sighed Dab-Dab. 'I've never stayed in a proper hotel before. I wonder what our room will be like?'

Their room was very pretty. It had a round window with seashell patterned curtains and a view over the tiny harbour. There was a little bed in the corner for the Doctor, and a big bed by the window for all the animals to share.

Gub-Gub squealed with delight as he noticed the pieces of cake the landlady had left for her guests, and the pushmi-pullyu sat on the bed trying to decide which way up to sleep.

Dab-Dab began bustling about, unpacking the luggage and checking under the beds for dust.

'Oh do stop fussing,' said Jip, jumping up at the window to admire the view. 'Why, Doctor,' he barked, wagging his tail in excitement, 'I can see Dora's boat from here.'

Emergency

After breakfast the next morning, they all set off for the beach. They packed some sandwiches and a bottle of lemonade, and Gub-Gub carried his bucket and spade. The sun was shining and very warm. Even the pushmi-pullyu was fanning himself, and Dab-Dab could hardly wait to get in the water.

'Come on, Doctor,' she cried. 'Let's go for a paddle! It's about time you had some fun.'

After they'd eaten their picnic, the Doctor settled back in his deck chair for an afternoon sleep. Dora arrived with her bat and ball and played with the animals until teatime.

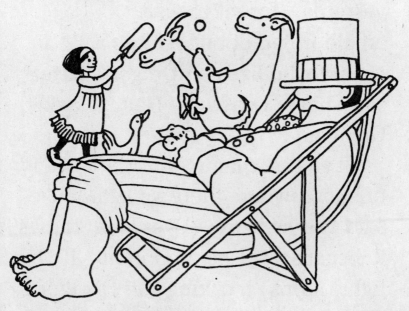

Just as it was beginning to get dark the swallow suddenly appeared and perched himself on the picnic basket.

'Doctor!' he said urgently. 'I've got something very important to tell you. After I left you yesterday, I went to visit an old friend of mine. She's a canary who lives on Dragon's Head.'

'What's Dragon's Head?' asked Gub-Gub.

'It's the name of the island offshore, where there's a lighthouse,' said the swallow. 'Everyone knows it because it's so important. If the light stops working on Dragon's Head, then all the boats are in danger.'

'Why?' asked Dab-Dab.

'Because the lighthouse warns

them that if they go any nearer to shore, they will be smashed on the Dragon Rocks,' explained the swallow.

'Anyway, Rita – that's the canary – was very pleased to see me and we had a good chat. Then she told me that she was very worried. "It's my owner," she said. "He's not well, I know it. He keeps having these dizzy spells. But he won't go to the doctor. One day he's going to fall over and then who is going to keep the light working?"

'I explained about you and we thought – I mean, I thought – that perhaps you would go and see this man and make sure there's nothing wrong with him.'

'It's a long time since I treated a human,' said the Doctor, 'but this man sounds as if he needs help. It's getting dark now but I'll set off first thing in the morning and visit him. Could I borrow your boat, Dora?'

'Certainly,' she said.

Where is the Dragon's Head Light?

That evening the Doctor was writing postcards by the light of a candle. It was late and all the animals were fast asleep in their new bed.

Suddenly he heard a tapping at the window. He put down his pen and drew back the curtains. There on the sill was the swallow looking very worried indeed.

'Doctor,' he panted, 'the Dragon's Head light has gone out. The night's as black as ink. And that's not the worst: there's a big sailing ship heading for the rocks and the sailors don't know what danger they're in. You must come at once.'

'Good Heavens!' cried the Doctor. 'The keeper must have collapsed. Wait a moment while I wake the others.'

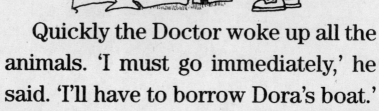

Quickly the Doctor woke up all the animals. 'I must go immediately,' he said. 'I'll have to borrow Dora's boat.'

'We're coming too,' said Dab-Dab

firmly. 'You'll need us. What if this lighthouse keeper is really ill? Someone will have to take a message.'

The Doctor wasn't very happy, but in the end he had to agree. He grabbed his little black medicine bag and calling to the animals to follow, he ran out of the hotel towards the *Lucky Lucy*.

When all the animals were in the boat (and it was a bit of a squeeze), the Doctor pushed off and began rowing towards the lighthouse.

It was very dark and the swallow

was having trouble guiding them. 'Where *is* this lighthouse?' grumbled Dab-Dab. 'We'll smash into the rocks ourselves if we're not careful.'

'Let me help,' said Too-Too the owl. 'I can see in the dark. I'll go and see where the ship is.'

He rose up into the air and was gone for about ten minutes. When he returned, he was in a panic.

'Doctor! Doctor!' he cried. 'The lighthouse is very close now. If you listen, you can hear the waves crashing on the rocks. And that ship is heading straight for them.'

'Oh, no,' groaned the Doctor,

'we're going to be too late!' and he
nearly broke the oars as he churned
the water to make the boat go faster.

'Listen, Doctor,' said the swallow.
'I've got a plan. Too-Too, you guide
the Doctor to the lighthouse. Dab-
Dab, come with me, I need your help.
I'll explain as we go.' And the two
birds flew off towards the ship,
leaving the Doctor rowing as hard as
he could in the darkness.

Bird Attack!

Unaware of the danger they were in, the sailors on the big ship were calmly sailing towards the rocks. One sailor was holding the ship's wheel and watching the compass swinging in front of him. He shook his head anxiously.

'Where's the Dragon Head Light? We should have seen it hours ago. Now – I must be seeing things! Is that a duck?'

Dab-Dab perched on the captain's cabin and quacked, 'Turn your ship! There are rocks ahead!'

'It's no good, he can't understand

you,' said the swallow. 'We'll have to stop this ship another way.' He flew into the wheelman's face and Dab-Dab covered the compass, so the sailor could not steer the ship.

The sailor, battling with the birds, let out a yell for help, saying he couldn't steer the ship. The Captain came running. Seeing that the sailor couldn't possibly steer with birds fluttering in his face, he gave the order to stop the ship and to get out the hose pipes.

Soon a strong jet of water was turned on the birds so they could no longer attack the wheelman.

'How dare you?' quacked Dab-Dab angrily. 'We're only trying to help.'

'It's no use,' said the swallow. 'We'll have to fly back to the Doctor. Let's hope he'll get the light working soon.' And the birds flew off again, shaking the water off their wings.

The Captain was very pleased. 'Well done, men,' he said. 'Now let's set sail again. The lighthouse can't be far.'

And slowly the ship began to head towards the rocks once more.

The Pushmi-Pullyu to the Rescue

Meanwhile Too-Too had guided the Doctor and the other animals safely past the rocks to the lighthouse. The Doctor sprang ashore and scrambled up the steep path in the dark. Feeling and fumbling he found the door and banged on it as hard as he could. There was no answer. He rattled the door handle. The door was locked.

'What shall we do?' said the Doctor worriedly. 'The keeper must be lying ill inside. Maybe he can't open the door! We've *got* to get inside! The question is, *how*?'

'Perhaps I can help?' said the pushmi-pullyu, shyly. 'Stand back everyone!'

'The other animals watched anxiously as the pushmi-pullyu pawed the ground. Then he lowered his horns and raced at the door.

CRUNCH! He hit it right next to the lock. The door shook, but it didn't break.

'Well done!' shouted the Doctor. 'Again!'

Six times the pushmi-pullyu ran at the door and crashed into it. On the seventh time, there was a splintering, cracking noise. The door gave way and the Doctor pushed inside.

'Hurry, everyone!' he cried. 'We've got to get that light working!' and he rushed up the winding stairs of the tower to the big lamp at the top.

It was dark inside the lighthouse. None of the animals could see a paw in front of their faces. Gub-Gub slipped on the stone stairs and trod on Jip's tail. At any minute they hoped to see the great beam of light from the lighthouse as the Doctor got it lit.

But instead, they suddenly heard the Doctor shouting from the top of the steps. 'I can't light it. I haven't got any matches.'

'What have you done with them?' asked Jip.

'You left them by your pipe at the hotel,' said Whitey, 'but there must be some matches somewhere in the lighthouse.'

All of a sudden, they heard a

canary singing.

'That must be the swallow's friend, Rita!' cried the Doctor. 'Rita, where are you?'

'Is that you, Doctor Dolittle?' sang the canary. 'I'm so glad to see you. I'm down here in the kitchen.'

Doctor Dolittle felt his way down the stairs to a small doorway. He took one careful step forwards – and his foot touched something warm. It was the body of a man lying on the floor!

'It must be the lighthouse keeper,' cried the Doctor. 'Quick! Fetch me some water, someone. And, Rita, where are the matches?'

'On the mantelpiece,' said the canary. 'Come over to my cage and feel along to your left – high up – and your hand will fall right on them.'

The Doctor sprang across the room, upsetting a chair. He felt along the shelf, and the animals gave a sigh of relief as they heard the rattle of the match box and saw the Doctor strike a match.

'You'll find a candle on the table behind you,' sang Rita.

The Doctor lit the candle and Gub-Gub carried a little mug of water over to the lighthouse keeper.

Then the Doctor bounded out of the room towards the stairs. 'Let's hope I'm not too late,' he cried.

And Then There was Light!

At that moment, Dab-Dab and the swallow flew in. 'We stopped the ship for as long as we could,' they cried. 'But then those silly sailors turned hoses on us and we had to give up. The ship is getting closer and closer.'

Without a word, the Doctor raced up the winding steps of the tower. Round and round he went until he felt quite dizzy. At last he reached the glass lamp, put down his candle and lit two matches at once. He held one in each hand and lit the wick in two places.

Whoosh! The lantern lit up so brightly that the Doctor was almost

blinded. A sharp beam of light cut across the waves, just in time. The front of the big sailing ship was only seconds away from the rocks.

The ship's look-out gave a cry of fear, and the Captain grabbed the wheel. Slowly, the big ship swung her nose out to sea and sailed safely past.

'We've done it!' yelled the Doctor, and the animals danced for joy.

Rita's Story

As soon as he was sure that the lighthouse lantern was properly alight, the Doctor went down to help the lighthouse keeper.

'I said that he kept getting dizzy spells,' said the canary. 'I knew something like this would happen.'

'You were quite right,' said the Doctor. 'It's a good thing you warned me.'

'He's waking up,' said Dab-Dab. 'See, his eyes are beginning to blink.'

'Get me some more clean water from the kitchen,' said the Doctor, who was bathing a large lump on the man's head.

Soon the keeper opened his eyes

wide and stared up into the Doctor's
face. 'Who? . . . What? . . .' he
murmured. 'The light! The light! I
must put on the light!' And he
struggled weakly to get up.

'It's all right,' said the Doctor. 'The light has been lit. Here, drink this. Then you'll feel better.' And he gave him some medicine which he had taken from his little black bag.

Soon the lighthouse keeper was well enough to stand up.

'We must get you to the hospital as soon as it's daylight,' said the Doctor. 'You've had a nasty shock.'

Rita helped them to pack a little bag for the lighthouse keeper. She wanted to come with them to the mainland, just to keep an eye on him. After Dab-Dab had made everyone some breakfast, the Doctor helped the keeper out to the *Lucky Lucy* which was still bobbing beside the rocks.

'Too-Too and I will fly back,' said Dab-Dab. 'I really don't think there's room for all of us.'

They made the keeper comfortable in the boat and put a blanket over his knees. Then the Doctor began to row back to Little Snoring.

'I'm looking forward to a little holiday,' said the keeper. 'It will be nice to see all my friends. The canary and me, we get a bit lonely out here.'

Welcome Back!

They hadn't gone far when they were met by several little boats, all out looking for them. Dora had raised the alarm when she'd noticed that her boat was missing and her friends were nowhere to be seen.

Doctor Dolittle explained what had happened and one of the boats went on ahead with the news that everyone was safe.

When they arrived back at Little Snoring, there was a big crowd on the beach. The brass band from the seafront was playing and everyone was waving flags.

'Goodness me!' said the Doctor. 'What's going on?'

'It's the welcome party,' Dora explained. 'It's because you saved the Dragon's Head Light.'

The next day, they all visited the lighthouse keeper in hospital. He was much better but he was worried about his lighthouse.

'Don't worry,' said the Doctor. 'The harbour master has already sent out someone to make sure that the light stays on. He'll look after it until you are ready to go back.'

Then the lighthouse keeper asked if the canary could stay with him, to keep him company. The nurses agreed and Rita was a great success. Her singing cheered up all the other sick people in the hospital, and Doctor Dolittle and the animals stayed there, laughing and talking, until evening.

Goodbye to Little Snoring

In the next few days, the Doctor and his animals enjoyed the rest of their holiday. They played on the sand, went exploring in the *Lucky Lucy* and had lots of fun. Dora even won a coconut on a coconut shy. Gub-Gub followed her with hopeful eyes until she broke it open and gave him the sweet milk inside.

'Do you realise,' said Dab-Dab to Jip, 'that we've only got one more day of our holiday left?'

'I'm beginning to miss Puddleby,' said Jip. 'I keep thinking of that bone I buried in the garden before we left. It must be just about right by now.'

On the last day, Dora's aunt made a picnic for everyone and they took it to the beach. They all paddled in the sea and afterwards they played Piggy in the Middle. Gub-Gub loved it but he got sunburned and had to sit under an umbrella with a cold cloth on his head.

Dora looked a little sad. 'I'm going to miss you all,' she said. 'It's been the best holiday I've ever had.'

'We'll miss you too,' said the Doctor.

Just then there was a twittering overhead from the swallow.

'What's he saying?' asked Dora.

'The Doctor smiled. 'He says that we'll all have to come back next year, just like he does!'